W9-AEH-570

Adventures of the Rat Family

THE IONA AND PETER OPIE LIBRARY OF CHILDREN'S LITERATURE

ADVENTURES OF THE RAT FAMILY

A Fairy Tale by

JULES VERNE

ILLUSTRATIONS BY FELICIAN MYRBACH-RHEINFELD

TRANSLATED BY EVELYN COPELAND

INTRODUCTION BY IONA OPIE

AFTERWORD BY BRIAN TAVES

OXFORD UNIVERSITY PRESS
NEW YORK   OXFORD

Oxford University Press

Oxford   New York   Toronto
Delhi   Bombay   Calcutta   Madras   Karachi
Kuala Lumpur   Singapore   Hong Kong   Tokyo
Nairobi   Dar es Salaam   Cape Town
Melbourne   Auckland   Madrid

and associated companies in
Berlin   Ibadan

Copyright © 1993 by Oxford University Press, Inc.

Published by Oxford University Press, Inc.,
200 Madison Avenue, New York, New York 10016

Oxford is a registered trademark of Oxford University Press

Library of Congress Cataloging-in-Publication Data
Verne, Jules, 1828-1905
[Aventures de la famille raton. English]
Adventures of the rat family / Jules Verne:
translated by Evelyn Copeland: introduction by Iona Opie: afterword by Brian Taves.
p. cm. — (The Iona and Peter Opie Library)
Summary: A good fairy must combat the efforts of a jealous prince and an evil genie
while she helps the members of a rat family in their quest to become human.
ISBN 0-19-508114-5
[1. Fairy tales. 2. Rats—Fiction.] I. Title. II. Series.
PZ8.V44Ad 1993
[Fic]—dc20   92-36983
CIP
AC

1 3 5 7 9 8 6 4 2

Printed in Singapore
on acid-free paper

INTRODUCTION

IONA OPIE

Jules Verne was born in the great French port of Nantes, on the Loire, in 1828, and he died at Amiens in 1905. He came from a legal and seafaring family and was himself educated for the law, but he refused to work seriously at anything but writing. In fact, writing ruled his life at the expense of personal happiness.

As a young man, studying law in Paris, he collaborated on the librettos of two operas, and in 1850 his verse comedy, *Les pailles rompues (The Broken Straws),* was produced at a Paris theater. He married a young widow with two small children and became a stockbroker. For some years his interests alternated between the theater and the stock exchange, but some imaginative adventure tales he wrote for the magazine *Musée des familles* revealed his true gift. From about 1863 he began to pour forth, in sympathy with the mid-19th-century interest in scientific discovery, the novels that brought him international fame.

None of Verne's adventure stories were written specifically for children, but they quickly became the favorite reading of young people of both sexes. His two best-loved stories are *Vingt mille lieues sous les mers (Twenty Thousand Leagues under the Seas),* published in 1870, and *Le tour du monde en quatre-vingts jours (Around the World in Eighty Days),* first published in 1872. Who can forget Captain Nemo of the Nautilus—an anticipation of the modern submarine—with his enthusiasm for ramming enemy ships; or Phileas Fogg, that ambitious traveler, and his imperturbable companion Passepartout?

In *Adventures of the Rat Family* we have another extraordinary voyage, this time involving a series of fascinating transformations. The French have, of course, long been masters of the art of the literary fairy tale, and here that art is enhanced by Jules Verne's sparkling style and his good-natured caricatures of contemporary upper-class society. The rats epitomize the elegance of late 19th-century France, and the mother, Ratonne, personifies its luxurious tastes.

The story hinges upon the workings of reincarnation. The rats are moved up and down the rungs of creation (becoming, for example, oysters, birds, or humans) by the good fairy Firmenta or the bad magician Gardafour, as in a game of Snakes and Ladders. The sudden transformations and surprising escapes that result are in the best Jules Verne manner.

Each member of the rat family has a distinctive character. The dissatisfied, vain mother, Ratonne, so constantly looks at herself in mirrors that they are "in danger of being worn out." Simple, honest Raton, the father, refuses the final honor of becoming a human being because "as the poet Menander said so many centuries ago, dog, horse, ox, donkey, all are preferable to being a man." Their daughter, Ratine, is everybody's idea of a charmingly pretty heroine. Her cousin, Raté, is the buffoon necessary in any successful story; his transformation never works out right, and he is always left with the wrong combination of parts.

"Listen then, my children," for this is a civilized and timeless tale, and from it you may gain much wisdom.

RATA
RATANE   RATONNE   RATON   RATINE
                                           RATÉ

ONCE UPON A TIME there was a family of rats: the father, Raton; the mother, Ratonne; their daughter, Ratine; and her cousin, Raté. Their servants were the cook, Rata, and the maid, Ratane.

Now, my dear children, these worthy, esteemed rodents had such extraordinary adventures that I cannot resist the desire to narrate them to you.

These adventures took place in the age of fairies and magicians, and also during the time that animals talked. Still, they didn't talk any more nonsense than did people of that epoch, nor any more than do people of today, for that matter. Listen, then, my dear children. I begin!

II

IN ONE OF THE most beautiful cities of that time, in the most beautiful house in the city, lived a good fairy. Her name was Firmenta. She did as much good as it is possible for a fairy to do, and she was greatly beloved. At that time, it appears, all living beings were subject to the transmigration of souls. Do not be frightened by this word; it means that there was a ladder of creation, and every living being had to climb the rungs in sequence in order to attain the final one and take his place in humanity. Thus, one was born a mollusk, then became a fish, a bird, a quadruped, and finally a man or a woman. As you see, it was necessary to climb from the most rudimentary state to the most perfect one. It could happen, however, that one *descended* the ladder, thanks to the evil influence of some magician. For example, after having been a man, one could become an oyster again! And then, what a sad existence! Fortunately, that doesn't happen nowadays—physically, at least.

You should know, also, that these metamorphoses were accomplished by genies as intermediaries. The good genies made one *ascend*, the bad ones made one *descend*, and if these latter abused their power, the Creator could deprive them of it for a certain time.

It goes without saying that the fairy Firmenta was a good genie, and no one ever had any occasion to complain about her.

One fine morning she found herself in the dining room of her palace—a room decorated with superb tapestries and magnificent flowers. The sun's rays shone in through the window, illuminating with bright, sparkling touches the porcelain and silver on the table.

The maid had just announced to her mistress that lunch was served—a fine lunch, to which fairies certainly had a right without being accused of gluttony. But hardly had the fairy seated herself when there was a knock at the door of the palace.

The servant went immediately to open the door; a moment later, she informed the fairy that a handsome young man wished to speak with her.

"Have this handsome young man enter," answered Firmenta.

He *was* handsome, in fact, above average in height, twenty-two years of age, with a fine, honest look. Very simply dressed, he presented himself gracefully. Immediately, the fairy formed a good opinion of him. She thought that he had come for help, as had so many others, and she felt disposed to oblige him.

"What do you want of me, handsome young man?" she said in her gentle voice.

"Good fairy," he answered, "I am most unhappy, and you are my only hope..." he hesitated.

"Explain yourself," Firmenta prompted. "What is your name?"

"It is Ratin," he answered. "I am not rich, but I have not come to ask for wealth. No, it is happiness that I seek."

"Do you think, then, that one can exist without the other?" replied the fairy, smiling.

"I do think so."

"And you are right. Continue, handsome young man."

"Sometime ago," he continued, "before becoming a man, I was a rat, and as such, was very well received by an excellent family to which I hoped to become attached by the sweetest of bonds. I was pleasing to the father, who is a very sensible rat. The mother

perhaps eyed me less favorably, because I am not rich. But their daughter, Ratine, regarded me so tenderly!…Anyway, I was doubtless going to be accepted, when a great misfortune cut short all my hopes!"

"What happened?" asked the fairy, with the most intense interest.

"First of all, I became a man, while Ratine remained a rat!"

"Well," answered Firmenta, "Wait for her final transformation, which will make her a young girl…"

"Of course, good fairy! Unfortunately, Ratine has been noticed by a powerful lord who may be the son of the king. Accustomed to indulging his fantasies, he does not tolerate the slightest opposition. Everything must yield to his wishes."

"And who is this lord?" asked the fairy.

"It is Prince Kissador. He proposed to my dear Ratine that she be brought to his palace, where she would be the happiest of rats. She refused, even though her mother, Ratonne, was very flattered by this proposal. The prince then tried to buy her for a very high price; but the father, Raton, knowing how much his daughter loved me, and that I would die of grief if we were separated, did not at all wish to consent. I will not even *try* to describe to you the fury of Prince Kissador. Seeing Ratine so beautiful as a rat, he told himself that she would be even more beautiful as a girl! Yes, good fairy, even more beautiful! And he would then marry her!…This was certainly very reasonable for him, and so unfortunate for us!"

"Undoubtedly," answered the fairy. "But since the prince was sent away, what have you to fear?"

"Everything," answered Ratin, "because, in order to get what he wants, he has appealed to Gardafour."

"That magician!" exclaimed Firmenta. "That evil genie who is happy only when he causes harm, and against whom I am always struggling?..."

"The very one, good fairy."

"This Gardafour, whose fearsome power seeks only to bring back to the bottom of the ladder the creatures who are raising themselves little by little toward the highest rank?"

"Exactly as you say!"

"Fortunately, Gardafour, having abused his power, has just been deprived of it for some time."

"That's true," answered Ratin, "but at the time that the prince appealed to him, he was still in complete possession of it. Enticed by the promises of this lord, and frightened by his threats, Gardafour promised to avenge him for the slight of the Raton family!"

"And did he do it?"

"He did it, good fairy!"

"How?"

"He metamorphosed those good rats! He changed them into oysters. And now they are vegetating on the banks of the Samobrives, where these mollusks, of excellent quality, I must say, are worth three francs a dozen, which is to be expected, since the Raton family is among them! You see, good fairy, the full extent of my misfortune!"

Firmenta listened with pity and kindness to the young man's story. She readily sympathized with human suffering, and especially with thwarted love.

"And so what can I do for you?" she asked.

"Good fairy," answered Ratin, "since my Ratine is attached to the bank of the Samobrives, make me into an oyster also, so that I may have the consolation of living there near her."

This was said with such a sad voice that Firmenta was very much moved, and she took the young man's hand.

"Ratin," she said, "I would like to grant you this wish, but I would not be able to succeed. You see, I am forbidden to make living beings descend the ladder of humanity. However, since I cannot reduce you to a mollusk, which is certainly a humble state, I can have Ratine climb back up."

"Oh, do it, good fairy, do it!"

"But she will have to go through the intermediate steps before becoming a charming rat again, destined to be a young girl one day. So be patient. Submit to the laws of nature. And have confidence also..."

"In you, good fairy?"

"Yes, in me. I will do everything to help you. Don't forget, however, that we will have to withstand violent struggles. You have in Prince Kissador, even though he is the most stupid of princes, a powerful enemy. And if Gardafour's power were restored before you became the beautiful Ratine's husband, it would be difficult for me to defeat him, because he would have become my equal again."

Then a little voice was heard—where was it coming from?—calling, "Ratin!...my poor Ratin...I love you!"

"It's Ratine's voice!" exclaimed the handsome young man. "Ah! Madame Fairy, Madame Fairy, have pity on her!"

Ratin was frantic. He ran across the room, he looked under the furniture, he opened the sideboards, thinking Ratine might be hidden there. But he couldn't find her.

The fairy stopped him with a gesture.

And then, my dear children, a singular event took place. On the table, arranged on a silver platter, were a half-dozen oysters that had come from the bank of the Samobrives. In the middle was the prettiest one, with her shining bordered shell. And she was growing, swelling, enlarging, developing, then opening wide. From the folds of her little collar emerged an adorable face, with corn blond hair, the sweetest, gentlest eyes in the world, a straight little nose, a charming mouth that kept saying:

"Ratin! My dear Ratin!"

"It is she!" exclaimed the handsome young man.

It was, in fact, Ratine. He had recognized her. Because I must tell you, dear children, that in that happy magic time, living beings already had human faces, even before being part of humanity.

And how beautiful Ratine was under her pearly shell, like a jewel in its case.

And she said:

"Ratin, my dear Ratin, I heard everything that you have just told Madame Fairy, and Madame Fairy has graciously promised to undo the evil that the wicked Gardafour has done to us. Oh, don't abandon me, because if he changed me into an oyster, it's so that I won't be able to flee. Then Prince Kissador will come and detach me from the bank to which my family is attached. He will carry me off, put me in his fish pond, wait until I become a girl, and I will be lost forever to my poor dear Ratin!"

She uttered these words so sadly that the young man,

profoundly moved, could hardly speak.

"Oh, my Ratine!" he murmured.

And in a burst of tenderness, he extended his hand toward her, but the fairy stopped him. She then delicately removed a magnificent pearl that had formed in the oyster:

"Take this pearl," she said to him.

"This pearl, good fairy?"

"Yes, it is worth a great fortune. It will be useful to you later. Now we will bring Ratine back to the bank of the Samobrives, and there I will have her ascend one rung..."

"Not alone, good fairy!" Ratine pleaded. "Think of my good father Raton, my good mother Ratonne, my cousin Raté! Think of our faithful servants Rata and Ratane!"

But while she was speaking, the two halves of her shell slowly reclosed and went back to their ordinary dimensions.

"Ratine!" cried the young man.

"Take her away," said the fairy.

Ratin pressed the shell to his lips. Did it not contain everything that was dearest in the whole world to him?

III

THE TIDE WAS LOW. The surf gently beat against the bank of the Samobrives. There were pools among the rocks, and the granite sparkled like polished ebony. When one walked on the viscous seaweed, its husks burst, and little jets of liquid spurted out. One had to be careful not to slip, for a fall would be painful.

What a large quantity of mollusks clung to this bank! Vine-like great snails, mussels, and especially oysters by the thousands. Half a dozen of the most beautiful were hiding under the marine plants. No, I am mistaken; there were only five. The space for the sixth was unoccupied!

Now the oysters were opening up to the sun's rays, breathing in the fresh air. At the same time there arose a plaintive chant, like a Holy Week litany.

The shells of these mollusks slowly parted. Between their transparent fringes appeared faces that were easy to recognize. One was Raton, the father, a philosopher, a sage, who knew how to accept life in all its forms.

"Undoubtedly," he thought, "having been a rat, being a mollusk again never stops being painful. But one must resign oneself to the inevitable and take things as they come."

In the second oyster was a face with a discontented grimace whose eyes flashed lightning. She tried, in vain, to hurl herself out of her shell. It was Lady Ratonne, and she said:

"To be shut up in this shell of a prison! I, who belonged to the highest rank in our city of Ratopolis! I, who, having arrived at the human phase, would have been a grande dame, a princess...perhaps...Ah! that wretched Gardafour!"

In the third oyster was the animal-like face of Raté, a real simpleton, cowardly, who cocked his ear at the slightest noise, like a hare. I must tell you that naturally, in his position as cousin, he had courted Ratine. But she, as we know, loved another, and Raté was extremely jealous of this other.

"Ah, ah!" he said. "What a fate! At least when I was a rat, I could run, escape, avoid the cats and the rat traps! But here I can be gathered, with a dozen of my peers, and the heavy knife of an oysterer can open me, brutally, and I will grace the table of some rich person, and I will be swallowed... alive...maybe!"

In the fourth oyster was the cook Rata, a chef extremely proud of his talents, very vain about his knowledge.

"That accursed Gardafour!" he exclaimed. "If I ever get him in one hand, I'll twist his neck with the other one. I, Rata, who accomplished so much, whose name has remained known, caught between two shells! And my wife Ratane..."

"Here I am," said a voice coming from the fifth oyster. "Don't aggravate yourself, my poor Rata! If I can't come closer to you, I am nonetheless at your side. And when you climb the ladder again, we will go up together!"

Good Ratane! Big and fat, very simple and modest, she loved her husband very much and, like him, was very devoted to her masters.

Then the sad litany began again, in a mood of gloom. Several hundred unfortunate oysters, also awaiting their deliverance, joined this concert of lamentations. It was heartrending. And what greater

grief for Raton, the father, and for Lady Ratonne, had they known that their daughter was no longer with them!

Suddenly all were quiet. The shells had reclosed.

Gardafour had just arrived. Dressed in his long magician's robe and wearing the traditional cap, he had a fierce look on his face. Near him walked Prince Kissador, richly dressed. You can't imagine how infatuated this lord was with himself, how ridiculously he moved in an effort to look graceful.

"Where are we?" he demanded.

"On the bank of Samobrives, my prince," Gardafour replied obsequiously.

"And this Raton family?"

"Still at the place where I attached them in order to please you!"

"Ah, Gardafour," replied the prince, twirling his mustache, "that little Ratine! I'm bewitched by her. She must be mine. I am paying you to serve me, and if you don't succeed, watch out!"

"Prince," answered Gardafour, "I was able to change this whole family of rats into mollusks, before my power was withdrawn, but then I could not change them into human beings; you know that."

"Yes, Gardafour, and that's exactly what enrages me so!"

Both of them stepped onto the bank, and at that moment two persons appeared on the other side of the shore. They were the fairy Firmenta and the young Ratin, who held to his heart the double shell that enclosed his beloved.

Suddenly they spotted the prince and the magician.

"Gardafour," said the fairy, "what are you doing here? Did you come to perpetrate another criminal act?"

"Fairy Firmenta," said Prince Kissador, "you know that I am crazy about the lovely Ratine. She is not wise enough to accept a gentleman of my quality, who awaits impatiently the hour when you will make her a young girl..."

"When I change her into a young girl," answered Firmenta, "it will be to belong to the one that she prefers."

"That impertinent one," retorted the prince, "that Ratin! Gardafour will not have to bother turning him into a donkey when I get through lengthening his ears!"

At this insult, the young man leaped up and was about to hurl himself on the prince to avenge his insolence, but the fairy seized his hand.

"Calm yourself," she said. "This is not the time for vengeance; the prince's insults will turn against him one day. Do what you have come to do, and let us leave."

Ratin pressed the oyster to his lips a last time, then put her down in the midst of her family.

Almost immediately, the tide began to cover the bank of the Samobrives. The water soon invaded the farthest peak, and everything disappeared as far as the horizon, where the sea merged with the sky.

IV

NEVERTHELESS, A FEW ROCKS remained uncovered. The tide cannot reach their summits, even when the storm propels the waves to the shore.

It was there that the prince and the magician took refuge. When the bank was again dry, they would look for the precious oyster that contained Ratine, and take her away. The prince was furious. Powerful as princes and kings are, they were powerless against fairies back then, and it would still be like that if we were ever to return to that happy time.

Firmenta spoke to the handsome young Ratin:

"Now that the sea is high, Raton and his family are going to reascend one rung toward humanity. I'm going to transform them into fish, and in this form they will have nothing more to fear from their enemies."

"Even from fishermen?" said Ratin.

"Be calm. I will watch over them."

Unfortunately, Gardafour overheard the fairy, and devised a plan. Followed by the prince, he made his way toward solid ground.

Then the fairy waved her wand toward the bank of the Samobrives, hidden under the waters. The oysters of the Raton family opened halfway. Wriggling fishes emerged, frisking about, joyously happy with this new transformation.

Raton, the father, was now a fine, dignified turbot with swellings on his brownish side. If he hadn't had a human face, he would have looked at you with his two great eyes placed on his left side.

Madame Ratonne, a weever with a thorny gill and a venomous dorsal fin, was nonetheless very beautiful because of her changing colors.

Mademoiselle Ratine, a pretty and elegant dorado, was almost diaphanous, very attractive in her raiment of mingled black, red, and azure.

Rata was a fierce ocean pike, with a long body, mouth split up to his eyes, sharp teeth, a furious look like a miniature shark, and an astonishing voracity.

Ratane had become a fat salmon trout, vermilion-colored, the two crescents of her eyes outlined against the silver background of her scales. She would have made a fine appearance on the table of some gourmet.

Finally, there was Cousin Raté, a whiting with a greenish-gray back. But by a freak of nature he was only half a fish! Yes, the extremity of his body, instead of ending in a tail, was still caught between two oyster shells! Wasn't that the height of the ridiculous? Poor cousin!

And now, under the clear waters, whiting, trout, pike, dorado, weever, and turbot drew up to the foot of the rock where Firmenta was waving her wand, and they seemed to say:

"Thank you, good fairy, thank you!"

V

AT THAT MOMENT, COMING from the open sea, was a sloop, with its large reddish foresail and jib set into the wind. It arrived in the bay, propelled by a fresh breeze. The prince and the magician were on board, and it was to them that the entire fishing catch was to be sold.

The trawl was dropped into the sea. This vast sack gathers from the sandy bottom hundreds of different kinds of fish—mollusks and crustaceans, crabs, shrimps, lobsters, dabs, skates, sole, brill, angel fish, weevers, dorados, turbot, bass, red mullet, red gurnet, gray mullet, surmullet, and many others.

Alas, what danger threatened the Raton family, just barely delivered from its shell prison! If by misfortune the trawl scooped it up, it would never be able to get out! Then the turbot, the weever, the pike, the trout, the whiting would be seized by the heavy hand of the sailors, thrown into the fishmongers' baskets, rushed to some great capital, displayed for sale, still palpitating, on the marble slabs of the retailers, while the dorado, carried off by the prince, would be forever lost to her beloved Ratin!

But here came a change in the weather. The sea swelled. The wind howled. The storm burst forth. It was a squall, a tempest!

The boat was horribly shaken by the waves. It didn't have time to lift up its trawl, which broke apart, and in spite of the helmsman's efforts, the boat was driven toward the shore and smashed to pieces on the reefs.

Prince Kissador and Gardafour escaped, thanks to the devotion of the fishermen.

It was the good fairy, my dear children, who had unleashed this storm for the salvation of the Raton family. She was always there, accompanied by the handsome young man, with her marvelous wand in her hand.

Now Raton and his family frisked about under the waters, which were becoming calm. The turbot turned and turned about, the weever swam coquettishly, the pike opened and closed his vigorous jaws, in which little fish were engulfed, the trout gave thanks, and the whiting, whose scales restrained him, moved about clumsily. As for the pretty dorado, she seemed to be waiting for Ratin to throw himself into the water to join her. Yes, he would have liked that, but the fairy restrained him.

"No," she said, "not until Ratine has returned to the form in which she first pleased you."

VI

RATOPOLIS, A VERY PRETTY city, is situated in a kingdom whose name I have forgotten, which is neither in Europe, nor in Asia, nor in Africa, nor in Oceania, nor in America, even though it is *somewhere*. In any case, the countryside around Ratopolis bears a strong resemblance to a Dutch landscape. It is fresh, and green, and clean, with clear streams, bowers shaded by beautiful trees, broad meadows where the most contented flocks in the world graze.

Like all cities, Ratopolis has streets, squares, and boulevards, but these boulevards, squares, and streets, are lined with magnificent cheeses in the form of houses: Gruyères, Edams, Goudas, twenty types of cheddar. Inside they are divided into floors, apartments, and rooms. Here live, as a republic, a large population of rats, wise, modest, and provident.

It was about seven o'clock one Sunday evening. Families of rats were promenading, enjoying the fresh air. They had worked hard all week to replenish the provisions of their households, and today they were resting.

Prince Kissador was in Ratopolis, accompanied by the ever-present Gardafour. They had learned that the members of the Raton family, after being fishes for some time, had become rats again, and

the two were now preparing secret traps for them.

"When I think," the prince kept saying, "that once again they owe their new transformation to that accursed fairy!"

"Ah! So much the better," replied Gardafour. "They will now be easier to catch. Fish can escape too easily. At present, they are rats, and we will be able to seize them. Once in your power," added the magician, "the beautiful Ratine will end up crazy about your lordship!"

At these words, the conceited idiot puffed out his chest and strutted about, ogling the pretty girl rats who were out walking.

"Gardafour," he said, "is everything ready?"

"Everything, my prince, and Ratine will not escape the trap I have set for her!"

Gardafour indicated an elegant cradle of leaves, set in the corner of the square.

"This bed hides a trap," he said, "and I promise you that this very day the beauty will be in your lordship's palace. There she will not be able to resist your charm and seduction."

And the imbecile swallowed the magician's exaggerated flattery.

"There she is," said Gardafour. "Come, my prince. She must not see us!"

They both made it to the next street.

Ratine was truly there, but Ratin was with her, accompanying her home. How charming she was, with her blond prettiness and her graceful figure! And the young man was saying to her:

"Ah! Dear Ratine, would that you were already a young girl! If only I could have become a rat again, in order to marry you immediately, I would not have hesitated. But that is impossible!"

"Oh, my dear Ratin, we must wait..."

"Wait! Always wait!"

"What does it matter, since you know that I love you and will never belong to anyone but you! Besides, the good fairy protects us, and we have nothing more to fear from the wicked Gardafour or from Prince Kissador..."

"That impertinent one," exclaimed Ratin, "that fool that I will punish!"

"No, my Ratin, no, don't quarrel with him! He has guards who would defend him! Have patience, since it is necessary, and confidence, since I love you!"

While Ratine was saying these things so gently, the young man pressed her to his heart and kissed her little paws.

And, as she felt a little tired after her walk:

"Ratin," she said, "over there is the little bed where I am in the habit of resting. Go to the house and inform my mother and father that they should meet me here to go to the festival."

And Ratine slid into the bed.

Suddenly there was a sharp, dry sound, like the creak of a spring loosening.

The foliage hid a perfidious rat trap, and Ratine, who could not have suspected it, had just touched the spring. Abruptly, a grating came down in front of the bed, and now she was caught!

Ratin uttered a cry of anger, which Ratine answered with a cry of despair, and which Gardafour answered with a cry of triumph. The magician came running with Prince Kissador.

The young man clung to the grid, trying to break the bars, but in vain. In vain was his desire to throw himself on the prince.

The best thing to do was find help to free the unhappy Ratine from her kidnapper, and that's what Ratin did as he escaped down the main street of Ratopolis.

Meanwhile, Ratine had been taken out of the rat trap, and Prince Kissador said to her most gallantly:

"I've got you, little one, and you will not escape from me again!"

VII

It was one of the most elegant houses in Ratopolis—a magnificent cheese from Holland—in which the Raton family lived. The living room, the dining room, the bedrooms, everything necessary for service—all was tasteful, and arranged for comfort. Raton and his family were counted among the most notable residents of the city, and enjoyed universal esteem.

This return to his former situation did not swell the heart of the worthy philosopher with pride. That which he had been, he would always be: modest in his ambitions, a truly wise man, whom La Fontaine would have made president of his rat council. One was well advised to heed his opinions. However, Raton was stricken with gout and could walk only with a crutch, when the gout did not confine him to his big armchair. He believed that vegetating for several months on the bank of the Samobrives had made his gout worse, even though he had been in waters reputed to be the best. This was especially unfortunate for him because—bizarre phenomenon—gout rendered him unsuitable for the final metamorphosis. In fact, that metamorphosis could never be performed on any individual suffering from this rich person's malady. Thus Raton would remain a rat for as long as he had the gout.

But Ratonne was not a philosopher. Here was her situation: when she became a lady at last, perhaps even a great lady, she would have as her husband a simple rat, and a gouty rat at that! One could die of shame! Thus she became more shrewish, more irritable than ever, picking quarrels with her husband, reprimanding her servants when orders were badly carried out (because they had been badly given), and making life difficult for the entire household.

"You must cure yourself, sir," she said to her husband, "and I will be able to make you do it!"

"I could ask for nothing better, my good wife," replied Raton, "but I'm afraid that's impossible. I will have to resign myself to remaining a rat."

"Rat! I, the wife of a rat! And what would I look like? Besides, there is our daughter in love with a fellow who doesn't have a cent! What a disgrace! Suppose I become a princess one day. Then Ratine will be a princess also..."

"In that case I will be a prince," replied Raton, not without a touch of malice.

"You, a prince, with a tail and paws! Look at the handsome lord!"

It was thus that all day long one heard Ratonne whining. Most often, she tried to vent her temper on poor cousin Raté, who continued to be a target for such abuse.

For once again the transformation had not been complete. Raté was a rat only by half—a rat in front, a fish in back, with the tail of a whiting, which made him absolutely grotesque. With this  condition, how could he hope to please the beautiful Ratine or even any of the other pretty rats of Ratopolis?

"What have I done to nature, that she treats me like this?" he cried. "What did I do?"

"Won't you please hide that ugly tail?" said Lady Ratonne.

"I can't, Aunt Ratonne."

"Well, then, cut it off, imbecile, cut it off!"

The cook, Rata, offered to do this operation, and then to use the whiting's tail in a superior recipe. What a treat it would be for a holiday!

Holiday at Ratopolis? Yes, my dear children! The Raton family planned to participate in a public celebration. They waited only for the return of Ratine.

At that moment, a coach arrived at the door of the house, bringing Firmenta, dressed in brocade and gold, to visit her protégés. If she smiled sometimes at the laughable ambitions of Ratonne, the ridiculous audacity of Rata, the stupidities of Ratane, and the lamentations of Cousin Raté, she thought very highly of the common sense of Raton, and she adored the charming Ratine. Firmenta devoted herself to the success of Ratine's marriage, and in her presence the Lady Ratonne didn't dare reproach the handsome young man for not being a prince.

Firmenta was therefore given a cordial welcome, with many thanks for all that she had done and would still do.

"Because we really need you, Madame Fairy!" said Ratonne. "Ah, when will I be a lady?"

"Patience, patience," answered Firmenta. "We must give nature a chance to work, and that requires a certain length of time."

"But why does nature want me to have a whiting's tail, even though I have become a rat again?" cried Cousin Raté, with a pitiful look on his face. "Madame Fairy, is it not possible to rid me of it?"

"Alas, no," replied Firmenta. "Truly, you are unlucky. That is probably due to your name, Raté, which means failure. Nevertheless you will certainly not have a tail when you become a bird!"

"Oh!" exclaimed Lady Ratonne. "How I wish to be an aviary queen!"

"And I, a beautiful fat turkey stuffed with truffles," said good Ratane naïvely.

"And I, a king of the farmyard!" added Rata.

"You will be what you will be," retorted Papa Raton. "As for me, I am a rat, and will remain one thanks to my gout. Better to be that, after all, than to turn up one's feathers, like so many birds of my acquaintance!"

At that moment, the door opened, and the young Ratin appeared, pale, defeated. In a few words, he related the affair of the rat trap, and how Ratine had fallen into the hands of the treacherous Gardafour.

"Ah! So that's how it is!" said the fairy. "You want to continue to fight, accursed magician! So be it! To the two of us!"

VIII

YES, MY DEAR CHILDREN, all Ratopolis was having a festival, and you would have enjoyed that very much, if your parents had been able to bring you there. Just think! Everywhere wide arches with transparent screens of a thousand colors, foliage curving over flag-bedecked streets, houses hung with tapestries, pyrotechnical devices crisscrossing in the air, music on every corner. And, you must believe me when I tell you that the rats could sing with the best choral societies in the world. They have sweet, sweet little voices, flute-like, of an ineffable charm. And, how they interpret the works of their composers: Rassini, Ragner, Rassenet, and so many other masters!

But what would have excited your admiration was a procession of all the rats of the universe, and of all those who, without being rats, were worthy of this significant name.

One could see rats who resembled Harpagon, carrying the miser's money box in their paws; hairy rats, soldiers of the old guard, whom war had made into heroes, always ready to cut the throat of the human race in order to win one more stripe; rats with tails on their noses, like elephants; church rats, humble and modest; wine-cellar rats, accustomed to poking their snouts into the merchandise; and especially fabulous numbers of nice dancing rats who perform the steps and countersteps of an opera ballet!

The Raton family approached this gathering of society, led by the fairy. But she saw nothing of this dazzling spectacle. She was thinking only of Ratine, poor Ratine, taken away from the love of her father and mother, as well as from the love of her fiancé!

Thus they arrived at the main square. The rat trap was still under the little bed, but Ratine was no longer there.

"Bring me back my daughter!" cried Lady Ratonne. Her only ambition now was to have her child returned, and it was truly pitiful to hear her.

The fairy tried in vain to conceal her anger against Gardafour, but it was obvious from her pinched lips and from her eyes, which had lost their customary gentleness.

A loud noise arose from the back of the square. A procession of princes, dukes, marquis, of the most magnificent lords, in superb raiment, was passing, preceded by armed guards of all types.

At the head of the principal group was Prince Kissador, distributing smiles and greetings to all those little people paying court to him.

Then, in the rear, in the midst of the servants, a poor, pretty little rat crawled along. It was Ratine, so guarded, so surrounded, that she could not think of fleeing. Her soft eyes, full of tears, said more than I can possibly tell you. Gardafour, walking near Ratine, didn't take his eyes from her. Ah! He really had her this time!

"Ratine...my daughter!" "Ratine...my betrothed!" Ratonne and Ratin tried in vain to reach her. The sneer with which Prince Kissador greeted the Raton family and the challenging glances that Gardafour flung at the fairy Firmenta were something to see. Even though he had been deprived of his magic power, he had triumphed, using only a simple rat trap.

All the lords were congratulating the prince on his new conquest. And with what conceit and self-satisfaction did the prince receive these congratulations!

Suddenly the fairy extended her arm, waved her wand, and a new metamorphosis took place.

Father Raton remained a rat, but Lady Ratonne was changed into a parakeet, Rata into a peacock, Ratane into a goose, and Cousin Raté into a heron. But, with his usual bad luck, instead of a

beautiful bird's tail he had a thin rat's tail that wagged under his plumage.

At the same moment, a dove rose lightly from the group of lords. It was Ratine!

You can just imagine the stupefaction of Prince Kissador, the anger of Gardafour! And then all of them, courtiers and servants alike, pursued Ratine, who escaped at full speed!

But the decor had changed. It was no longer the great square of Ratopolis; it was a beautiful landscape, in a

setting of tall trees, and from all over the sky a thousand birds came to welcome their new brothers of the air.

The Lady Ratonne, proud of her plumage, cackling happily, indulged in the most graceful frolicking, while good Ratane, painfully embarrassed, didn't know where to hide her goose feet.

As for Rata—Master Rata, if you please—he was strutting, showing off, as if he had been a peacock all his life, while the poor cousin murmured in a low voice, "Failed again...still a failure!"

But here came a dove flying through the air, uttering joyous little cries. Descending in elegant curves, she came to rest lightly on the shoulder of the handsome young man.

It was the charming Ratine, and she could be heard beating her wings and murmuring into the ear of her beloved:

"I love you, my Ratin, I love you!"

IX

WHERE ARE WE, MY dear children? Still in one of those countries that I don't know, and whose name I couldn't tell you. But this one, with its vast landscapes framed by trees from the tropics, growing against a very blue sky, looks like India, and its inhabitants like Hindus.

Let's enter this caravansary, a sort of immense inn, open to all comers. This is where the whole Raton family was reunited. Following the counsel of the fairy Firmenta, the family had begun traveling. The safest thing, they had decided, was to leave Ratopolis in order to escape the prince's vengeance, for they were not strong enough to defend themselves. Ratonne, Ratane, Ratine, Rata, and Raté were still only simple winged creatures. Let them become wild beasts, and it would no longer be so easy to get the better of them!

Yes, mere fowls, among whom Ratane was one of the least favored. She walked around alone in the courtyard of the inn.

"Alas! Alas!" she cried. "I was once an elegant trout, and then a rat who knew how to be pleasing. And now to have become a goose, a domestic goose, one of those farmyard geese that any old cook can stuff with chestnuts!"

And she sighed at this idea, adding:

"Who knows if even my husband hasn't thought of doing it? He scorns me now. How can you expect such a majestic peacock to have the slightest consideration for such a common, ordinary goose! If only I were a turkey! But no! And Rata is still not pleased with me!"

That appeared only too obvious when Rata came into the courtyard. But then, what a handsome peacock! He shook his light and mobile aigrette, painted with the most brilliant colors. He ruffled his feathers, which seemed to be embroidered with flowers and laden with precious stones. He fanned his superb plumage with its silken beard covering his tail feathers. How could such a wonderful bird lower himself before this goose, so unattractive under her ash-colored gray down and her brown coat?

"My dear Rata!" she said.

"Who dares to pronounce my name?" answered the peacock.

"I."

"A goose! What goose is this?"

"I am your Ratane!"

"Ah! What a horror! On your way, I beg you!"

"Really, vanity makes one utter such foolishness!"

The example for this came to the arrogant peacock from on high. Did his mistress display any better sense? Didn't she also treat her spouse disdainfully?

And just then there she was, making her entry, accompanied by her husband, her daughter, Ratin, and Cousin Raté.

Ratine was ravishing as a dove, with her bluish-gray plumage, her green neck gilded with delicate, changing hues, her breast Venetian red, and a delicate white mark on each wing.

How Ratin devoured her with his eyes! And what melodious cooing could be heard as she fluttered around the handsome young man!

Father Raton, leaning on his crutch, looked at his daughter admiringly. But Lady Ratonne found that she herself was even more beautiful!

Ah! How well nature had done with the parakeet metamorphosis! She chattered and chattered! She arranged her tail in tiers so as to make Master Rata himself jealous. You should have seen her when she placed herself in a ray of sunshine to make the yellow down of her neck shimmer and sparkle, when she shook her green feathers and her bluish wings! She was, in fact, one of the most wonderful specimens of Oriental parakeets.

"Well, are you content with your destiny, my good wife?" asked Raton.

"There is no more 'good wife' here," she replied sharply. "I beg you to control your expressions, and to remember the distance that now separates us."

"Me! Your husband?"

"A rat the husband of a parakeet? You're crazy, my dear!"

And Lady Ratonne puffed out her chest, while Rata spread his tail near her.

Raton made a little gesture of kindness to her servant, who had not lost esteem in his eyes. Then he said to himself:

"Ah, women, women! Do you see how vanity turns their heads? And even when it doesn't...But let's be philosophical."

And, during this family scene, what was happening to Cousin Raté, whose appendage didn't even belong to his species? After having been a rat with a whiting's tail, here he was, a heron with a rat's tail! If things continued like that, it would be deplorable! Therefore, he remained there, in a corner of the courtyard, perched on one foot, as thoughtful herons do, showing the front of his body whose whiteness stood out from the little black vertebrae, his ash-gray plumage and his turned-down crest behind.

Then the question arose of continuing the trip, in order to see and admire the country in all its beauty.

But Lady Ratonne admired only herself, and Master Rata admired only himself. Neither one nor the other looked at these incomparable landscapes, preferring cities and large villages in which to show off their charms.

While the voyage was being discussed, a new personage appeared at the gate of the inn.

He was one of the guides of the country, dressed in the Hindu fashion, and had come to offer his services to the travelers.

"My friend," Raton asked him, "what is there of unusual interest to see?"

"A marvel without equal," answered the guide, "the great sphinx of the desert."

"Of the desert!" exclaimed Lady Ratonne contemptuously.

"We certainly didn't come to visit a desert," added Master Rata.

"Oh!" answered the guide. "It won't be a desert today because it's the festival of the sphinx, and people are coming from all corners of the world to worship him."

This was enough to convince our conceited birds to visit. And it mattered little to Ratine and her fiancé where they were taken, provided they went there together. As for Raté and the good Ratane, the depths of a desert seemed to be an excellent refuge.

"Let's go!" said Lady Ratonne.

"Let's go!" answered the guide.

A moment later, everyone had left the inn, not suspecting that this guide was the magician Gardafour, unrecognizable in his disguise, luring them into a new trap

X

WHAT A SUPERB SPHINX, infinitely more beautiful than those sphinxes of Egypt, famous though they were! It was called the sphinx of Romiradour, and it was the eighth wonder of the universe.

The Raton family had just arrived at the edge of a vast plain, surrounded by dense forests and dominated in the distance by a chain of snow-covered mountains.

In the middle of the plain was an animal carved in marble. He was lying on the grass, facing straight ahead, his front paws extended, his body stretched out like a hillside. He measured at least five hundred feet in length and was one hundred feet wide, and his head rose eighty feet above the ground.

This sphinx has the same inscrutable look that characterizes his colleagues. He has never revealed the secret that he has kept for thousands of centuries. Nevertheless his vast brain is open to whoever wishes to visit it. One enters by a door between his paws. Interior stairways give access to his eyes, his ears, his nose, his mouth, and into the forest of hair that covers his skull.

In addition, in order to give you a good idea of the enormity of this monster, I must tell you that six people can comfortably fit into one of his eyesockets, thirty in each of the openings of his ears, forty in his nostrils, sixty in his mouth, where you could give a ball, and about a hundred in that head of hair as dense as a forest in America. So people come from all over, not to consult him, since he doesn't want to answer, for fear of making a mistake, but to visit him, as is done with the statue of St. Charles on one of the islands in Lake Maggiore.

You will permit me, my dear children, to refrain from dwelling any longer on the description of this marvel that does such honor to the genius of man. Neither the pyramids of Egypt, nor the Hanging Gardens of Babylon, nor the Colossus of Rhodes, nor the lighthouse of Alexandria, nor the Eiffel Tower can be compared to it. When the geographers finally decide on the region where the great Sphinx of Romiradour is located, I trust that you will visit it during your vacation.

But Gardafour knew it very well, and that's where he took the rat family. He had vilely deceived them by claiming that a great gathering of people would be there. The peacock and the parakeet were going to be very disappointed, for they cared nothing about the superb sphinx.

As you are probably thinking, the magician and Prince Kissador had made a plan, so the prince was there also, on the edge of a neighboring forest, with one hundred of his guards. As soon as the family entered the sphinx, they would be caught as if in a rat trap. If a hundred men couldn't succeed in capturing five birds, one rat, and a young lover, it would have to be because they were protected by some supernatural power.

The prince paced up and down, waiting for them. He was obviously most impatient, for previous schemes to capture the beautiful Ratine had been defeated. Ah! If only Gardafour had regained his power, what vengeance he could have wreaked on this family! But the magician was still reduced to powerlessness for a few more weeks.

This time, however, all the measures had been so well planned that surely neither Ratine nor her family would escape the wiles of their persecutor.

At that moment Gardafour, at the head of the little party of tourists, and the prince, surrounded by his guards, stood ready to act.

XI

FATHER RATON WALKED WITH a firm step, in spite of his gout. The dove, describing wide circles in the air, came to perch from time to time on Ratin's shoulder. The parakeet flitted from tree to tree, looking for the promised multitude. The peacock kept his tail carefully folded, so as not to tear it on the thorns, while Ratane waddled on her big feet. Behind them the heron, his beak low, struck violently, in a rage, at the air with his rat's tail. He had tried to stuff it into his pocket—I mean to say under his wing—but he had to give up on that because it was too short.

Finally, the travelers arrived at the feet of the sphinx. They had never seen anything so beautiful.

However, Lady Ratonne and Master Rata questioned the guide:

"And where is this great gathering of people that you promised us?"

"As soon as you have reached the head of the monster," replied the magician, "you will see over the crowd and be visible for several leagues in all directions."

"Well, then, let us enter, quickly!"

All of them penetrated into the interior, suspecting nothing. They didn't even notice that the guide had remained outside, closing behind them the door between the paws of the gigantic animal.

A half-light entering through the openings in the face made the stairways visible. After a few moments one could see Raton strolling between the lips of the sphinx, Lady Ratonne fluttering on the end of the nose, where she indulged in the most coquettish frolicking, Master Rata on top of the skull, strutting and showing off in a way that eclipsed the rays of the sun.

The young Ratin and Ratine stood in the right ear, whispering sweetly to each other.

Ratane was in the right eye, where her modest plumage would not be seen, and Cousin Raté was in the left eye, concealing his lamentable tail.

From these diverse points of the face, the Raton family was well positioned to contemplate the splendid panorama that unfolded up to the farthest limits of the horizon.

The weather was superb. Not a single cloud was in the sky, not a bit of haze on the ground.

Suddenly an animated crowd appeared at the edge of the forest. It advanced, it approached. Was this, then, the multitude of worshipers of the sphinx of Romiradour?

No! These were people armed with pikes, sabers, bows, and crossbows, marching in close formation. They could have only evil intentions.

In fact, Prince Kissador was at their head, followed by the magician, who had taken off his guide's clothing. The rat family knew it was lost unless those of its members with wings took flight.

"Flee, my beloved Ratine!" her fiancé cried. "Flee! Leave me in the hands of these despicable characters!"

"Abandon you? Never!" answered Ratine.

And besides, that would have been very imprudent. An arrow could have pierced the dove, as well as the parakeet, the peacock, the goose, and the heron. It was wiser to hide in the depths of the sphinx. Perhaps they could escape at night, by some secret passage, without fear of the prince's archers.

Ah! How regrettable that the fairy Firmenta had not accompanied her protégés on this trip!

Meanwhile, the young man had an idea, and a very simple one, like all good ideas: to barricade the door from the inside. This was done without delay.

It was just in time. Prince Kissador, Gardafour, and the guards had halted a few steps from the sphinx and now called on the prisoners to surrender.

An emphatic "No!" issuing from the lips of the monster was the only answer they received.

The guards hurled themselves against the gate, assaulting it with enormous blows. Surely it would yield very soon!

But then a light mist enveloped the sphinx's hair, and the fairy

Firmenta, emerging from its vapors, appeared atop Romiradour's head.

At this miraculous apparition, the guards recoiled. But Gardafour recalled them to the assault, and the wooden door began to give way under their blows.

At that moment the fairy lowered toward the ground the wand that was trembling in her hand...

What an unexpected eruption came through the broken door!

A tigress, a bear, a panther threw themselves on the guards. The tigress was Ratonne, with her tawny coat. The bear was Rata, with his fur bristling, his claws extended. The panther was Ratane, who sprang terrifyingly. This last metamorphosis had transformed the three winged creatures into savage beasts!

At the same time, Ratine was changed into an elegant doe, and Cousin Raté took the form of a donkey, which brayed in a terrible voice. But what an evil fate! He had kept his heron's tail, and it hung at the end of his rump! Escaping his destiny was clearly not possible for Raté!

Meanwhile, at the sight of the three formidable wild animals, the guards didn't hesitate a moment; they fled as if pursued by fire. There was nothing to keep them there, since Prince Kissador and Gardafour had set them the example. To be eaten alive didn't suit them, apparently.

The prince and the magician were able to reach the forest, but some of their guards were less fortunate. The tigress, the bear, and the panther had succeeded in barring their path. The poor devils could think only of seeking refuge inside the sphinx, and soon they could be seen coming and going inside its vast mouth.

By the time they realized what a bad idea this was, it was too late.

For the fairy Firmenta again extended her wand, and frightful roarings spread like claps of thunder through the air.

The sphinx had been changed into a lion.

And what a lion! His mane bristled, his eyes flashed fire, his formidable jaws opened, closed, and began their work of chewing. A moment later Prince Kissador's guards were pulverized by the teeth of the tremendous animal.

Then the fairy Firmenta jumped lightly to the ground. The tigress, the bear, and the panther came and crouched at her feet, like the savage beasts at the feet of their trainer who holds them with his eyes.

And since that epoch, the sphinx has become the lion of Romiradour.

XII

A CERTAIN AMOUNT OF time has passed. The Raton family had attained human form except for the father, still as gouty as he was philosophical, who had remained a rat. Others in his place would have been resentful, would have cried out at the injustice of fate, cursed their existence. He was content to smile, happy, he said, not to have to change any of his habits.

Be that as it may, rat though he was, he was also a rich lord. Since his wife would not consent to live in his old cheese house in Ratopolis, he occupied a sumptuous palace in a big city, the capital of still another unknown country, without being any prouder because of that. Pride, or rather vanity, he left to his wife, Ratonne, who had become a duchess and paraded around her quarters, looking at herself so much in the mirrors that they were in danger of wearing out.

On this day Duke Raton brushed his coat with the greatest care, and did as much grooming as one could expect of him. As for the duchess, she decked herself out in her most beautiful finery: a robe in a floral pattern, made of crushed velvet, crêpe de Chine, soft Indian silk, plush, satin, brocade, and watered silk; a Henry II corsage; a train embroidered with jet, sapphires, and pearls, several yards long, replacing the various tails she had worn before becoming a woman; diamonds that flashed fire, laces that the skillful Arachne could not have made finer or richer, a Rembrandt hat on which a bed of flowers was ranged in tiers—in short, everything was in the latest fashion.

But, you ask, why all this luxurious preparation? Here is why:

That day, in the palace chapel, the marriage of the charming Ratine and Prince Ratin would be celebrated. Yes, he had become a prince, to please his mother-in-law. How? By buying a principality. Now principalities, even though they are falling in price, are still quite expensive, without a doubt. Therefore, Ratin had devoted to this acquisition a part of the price of the pearl—you certainly haven't forgotten the famous pearl found in Ratine's oyster, worth millions!

He was rich, then. But wealth had not changed his tastes or those of his fiancée, who would become a princess when she married him. No! Even though her mother was a duchess, she was still the modest young girl that you know, and the prince was more in love with her than ever. She was absolutely beautiful in her white gown adorned with garlands of orange blossoms.

Naturally the fairy Firmenta planned to attend the wedding, which was her work to some degree, after all.

It was, then, a great day for the whole family. And Master Rata was superb. In his status as ex-chef, he had become a politician. There was no finer garment than his peer's suit, which must have been very expensive, because, by reversing it, it could be made into a senator's suit—and that could be very advantageous.

Ratane was no longer a goose, to her great satisfaction: she was a lady to be escorted. Her husband had been forgiven for his former disdain. He was once more completely hers, and was even a bit jealous of the gentlemen who hovered around his wife.

As for Cousin Raté...but he will be coming in soon, and you can contemplate him at your ease.

The guests gathered in the great drawing room that was brilliantly lit, perfumed with flowers, furnished in the richest, most elegant style, and draped with tapestries the likes of which are no longer made. People had come from the vicinity to attend the marriage of Prince Ratin. The great lords, the great ladies wanted to be part of the wedding procession for this charming couple.

An official announced that all was ready for the ceremony, and the marvelous parade began, accompanied by harmonious music.

The parade of these important personages required not less than an hour. Finally, in one of the last groups, Cousin Raté appeared. He was a very attractive young man indeed, dressed in the latest fashion: a courtier's coat, a hat adorned with a magnificent feather that swept the ground with each greeting.

The cousin had become a marquis, if you please, and was certainly no stain on the family. He had a very nice appearance, and presented himself with grace. Naturally, he did not lack for compliments, which he received with a certain modesty. One could observe, however, a certain sadness in his countenance, and his somewhat embarrassed bearing. He lowered his eyes deliberately and looked away from those who approached him. Why this reserve? Wasn't he a man now, as well as any duke or prince of the court?

There he was among those of his rank in the procession, marching rhythmically, at a ceremonial pace. Arriving at the corner of the drawing room, he turned to go back up...but how horrible!

Between the panels of his suit, under his courtier's coat, hung a tail, a donkey's tail. Raté tried in vain to hide this shameful remainder of his previous form!...It is said that he will never get rid of it!

You see, my dear children, when one gets a bad start in life, it is very difficult to find the right course again. The cousin is henceforth a man. He has attained the final degree. He cannot look forward to a new metamorphosis that will deliver him from this tail. He will keep it until his last sigh.

Poor Cousin Raté!

XIII

THUS THE MARRIAGE OF Prince Ratin and Princess Ratine was celebrated with the utmost magnificence, a fitting ceremony for this handsome young man and this beautiful young woman who were so well suited to each other!

The procession returned from the chapel in the same order, still proper, still as correct in its bearing, with a nobility of manner that is seen only in the upper classes, it seems.

If one objects, pointing out that all these lords are still only parvenus, having passed, by metamorphosis, through many humble phases, that they have been mollusks without minds, fishes without intellect, birds without brains, quadrupeds without reasoning ability, I will answer that one should hardly be surprised at finding them so proper. Besides, good manners can be learned, like history or geography. Nevertheless, considering what he might have been in the past, man would do better to behave more modestly, and humanity would gain thereby.

After the marriage ceremony, there was a splendid feast in the great hall of the palace. To say that the guests ate ambrosia prepared by the foremost chefs of the century, that they drank nectar drawn from the best wine cellars of Olympus, would not be saying enough.

Finally, the celebration ended with a ball, during which costumed dancing girls from India and Egypt amazed the august assembly.

Prince Ratin, as is proper, had opened the ball with Princess Ratine in a quadrille. The Duchess Ratonne appeared on the arm of a lord of royal blood, while Master Rata participated with an ambassadress. Ratane was escorted by the very own nephew of a Grand Elector.

As for Cousin Raté, he hesitated a long time before risking his skin. Even though it cost him dearly to stand aside, he didn't dare invite the charming women to whom he would have so happily offered his arm, not just his hand. At last, he decided to invite a delightful countess, of remarkable distinction, to dance. This amiable woman accepted, a little frivolously, perhaps, and the new couple launched into the whirlwind of a waltz by Gung'l.

Ah! What consequences! The room could not contain them! In vain did Cousin Raté try to gather up his donkey tail under his arm, as the waltzing ladies did with their trains. This tail, carried away by a centrifugal motion, escaped him, becoming more flexible, like a whip. It lashed the dancing groups, twisting itself around their legs and causing very dangerous falls, including, finally that of the Marquis Raté and the charming countess. She had to be carried away, half-fainting with shame, while the cousin fled at top speed.

This ludicrous episode ended the celebration, and everyone withdrew at the moment when dazzling showers of fireworks invaded the black depths of the night.

XIV

THE CHAMBER OF PRINCE Ratin and Princess Ratine was certainly one of the most beautiful in the palace. Didn't the prince think of it as a jewel case for the invaluable treasure that he possessed? That was where the young husband and wife were to be conducted, with great ceremony.

But before they could be brought there, two personages were able to gain entry.

Now, these two characters—you guessed it—were Prince Kissador and the magician Gardafour.

And here is their dialogue:

"You know what you promised me, Gardafour."

"Yes, my prince, and this time nothing can prevent me from

kidnapping Ratine for Your Highness."

"And when she becomes Princess Kissador, she will have no occasion to regret it."

"I agree," answered the flatterer Gardafour.

"You are sure of succeeding today?"

"You be my judge," replied Gardafour, pulling out his watch. "In three minutes, the time during which I was deprived of my magic powers will have elapsed. In three minutes my wand will once again be as powerful as that of the fairy Firmenta. If Firmenta was able to raise the members of that Raton family to the rank of human beings, I can bring them back down again to the level of the most common animals!"

"Fine, Gardafour, but I understand that Ratin and Ratine won't be alone in this room for a single moment!"

"They won't remain here, if I have recovered all my power before they arrive!"

"How much time is left now?"

"Two minutes..."

"There they are!" cried the prince.

"I'm going to hide in this closet," said Gardafour, "and I will appear as soon as it is time. You, my prince, withdraw, but remain behind this big door, and don't open it until I cry out, 'Your turn, Ratin!'"

"Agreed, and, above all, don't spare my rival!"

"You will be satisfied."

You can see the danger that still threatened this honest, decent family, so sorely tried already, and who could not suspect that the prince and the magician were so near!

XV

THE YOUNG HUSBAND AND wife had just been conducted to their chamber with great ceremony. The Duke and Duchess Raton accompanied them, along with the fairy Firmenta, who did not want to leave the handsome young man and the beautiful young girl whose love she had protected. Surely they have nothing more to fear from Prince Kissador, or from the magician Gardafour, who had never been seen in the country. Nevertheless, the fairy felt a certain anxiety, a secret foreboding. She knew that Gardafour was about to recover his magic power, and that did not cease to worry her.

Ratane was there, of course, offering her services to her young mistress, and also Master Rata, who didn't abandon his wife anymore, and also Cousin Raté, even though the sight of the one he loved must have been breaking his heart.

Meanwhile the fairy Firmenta, still anxious, was in a hurry for one thing only: to see if Gardafour wasn't hiding somewhere, behind a curtain, under a piece of furniture. She looked. No one!

So, now that Prince Ratin and Princess Ratine would remain in the chamber, very much alone, she regained her confidence completely.

Suddenly, a side door opened abruptly, at the moment that the fairy was saying to the young couple:

"Be happy!"

"Not yet!" cried a terrible voice.

Gardafour appeared, shaking his magic wand. Firmenta could do nothing more for this unfortunate family!

They were all struck dumb. They stood motionless at first, then drew back, pressing themselves around the fairy as they faced the fearsome Gardafour.

"Good fairy," they repeated, "have you abandoned us? Good fairy, protect us!"

"Firmenta," said Gardafour, "you have exhausted your power to save them, and I have regained all of mine to ruin them! Your wand can now do no more for them, while mine…"

As he spoke, Gardafour waved his wand in circles, and it hissed in the air as if it had been endowed with a supernatural existence.

Raton and his family realized that the fairy was disarmed, that she could no longer protect them with a higher metamorphosis.

"Fairy Firmenta," cried Gardafour, "you have turned them into humans! And, I will turn them into beasts!"

"Mercy! Mercy!" whispered Ratine, holding out her hands toward the magician.

"No mercy!" replied Gardafour. "The first one among you to be touched by my wand will be changed into a monkey."

That said, Gardafour advanced on the unfortunate group as they fled in all directions.

They ran through the room but could not escape because the doors were closed. Ratin pulled Ratine along, trying to make a bulwark of his body for her, without thinking of the danger that threatened him.

Yes! Peril for himself, because the magician had just cried out:

"As for you, handsome young man, soon Ratine will only look upon you with disgust!"

At these words, Ratine fell senseless into the arms of her

mother. Ratin ran to the big door, but Gardafour rushed after him:

"For you!" he exclaimed.

And he lunged at Ratin with the magic wand, delivering a blow as if with a sword...

At that instant, the big door opened and Prince Kissador appeared, and it was he who received the blow intended for the young Ratin! It was Prince Kissador who was touched by the wand, and he was now a horrid chimpanzee!

To what fury he abandoned himself! He, so vain about his beauty, so full of pride, such a braggart, was now a monkey with a grimacing face, long ears, protruding snout, arms hanging down to his knees, a squashed nose, a yellowish skin with bristling hairs.

There was a mirror on one of the panels in the room. He looked at himself and uttered a terrible cry! He hurled himself at Gardafour, who was stunned by this bungling! Seizing him by the neck, Kissador strangled him with his strong chimpanzee's hand's.

Then the floor opened, as it usually does in all fairy tales. A vapor rose from the opening, and the wicked Gardafour disappeared in a fiery whirlwind.

As for Prince Kissador, he pushed out a window, cleared it in one leap, and ran off to join his fellow creatures in the neighboring forest.

XVI

And so I will surprise no one when I say that all that of this has ended in an apotheosis, in a dazzling setting, with the complete satisfaction of the senses of sight, hearing, smell, and even of taste. The eye admires the most beautiful sites in the world, under an Oriental sky. The ear is filled with the harmonies of Paradise. The nose smells intoxicating perfumes, distilled from billions of flowers. The lips are sweetened by air laden with the savor of the most delicious fruits.

In short, the whole happy family is in ecstasy, to the point that Raton, the father Raton himself, doesn't feel his gout anymore. He is cured, and thrusts his good crutch away angrily!

"Ah!" exclaims the Duchess Ratonne. "You don't have the gout anymore, my dear?"

"So it seems," says Raton. "I am rid of it…"

"Father!" exclaims Princess Ratine.

"Ah! Monsieur Raton!" Rata and Ratane add.

The fairy Firmenta approaches immediately, saying:

"Indeed, Raton, it's now up to you to become a man, and if you wish, I can…"

"A man, Madame Fairy?"

"Oh, yes!" retorts Lady Ratonne. "A man and a duke, as I am a woman and a duchess!"

"My word, no!" answers our philosopher. "Rat I am and rat I will remain, and as the poet Menander said so many centuries ago, dog, horse, ox, donkey, all are preferable to being a man, with all due deference to you."

XVII

THAT, MY DEAR CHILDREN, is the end of this story. From now on the Raton family no longer has anything to fear, neither from Gardafour, strangled by Prince Kissador, nor from Prince Kissador, who can no longer adore himself.

It follows, then, that they will be very happy, and will enjoy complete, untroubled good fortune.

Besides, the fairy Firmenta feels a real affection for them, and will not deprive them of her blessings and kindnesses.

Only Cousin Raté has some right to complain, since he has never attained a complete metamorphosis. He can't resign himself: that donkey's tail is his despair. He tries to cover it up...in vain! It always gets out.

As for simple, honest Raton, he will be a rat for the rest of his life, in spite of the duchess Ratonne, who reproaches him unceasingly for his refusal to be elevated to the rank of humans. And when the shrewish grande dame plagues him with too many recriminations, he contents himself by repeating, and applying to her, the words of the fabulist:

"Ah! Women! Women! Beautiful heads often, but brains, none at all!"

As for Prince Ratin and Princess Ratine, they are very happy, and have many children.

This is the way fairy tales usually end, and I will abide by it because it is best.

AFTERWORD

BRIAN TAVES

Adventures of the Rat Family is very different from the conventional expectation of a Jules Verne story. Verne's name conjures up images of a trip around the world in 80 days, an undersea voyage covering 20,000 leagues, and journeys to the center of the earth and around the moon. Verne's global popularity began with his first novel in 1863 and continues to this day. He is one of the all-time best-selling authors; no other novelist has been so widely translated and been read so much over such a long period. Verne is known as the prophet of the 20th century, inspiring those who would go to the moon, visit the poles, and build submarines and flying machines. Indeed, Verne is more than simply an author; he is a phenomenon whose influence has radiated throughout science and the arts.

Despite Verne's fame, he is often misunderstood, and a century's worth of myths and misconceptions have become attached to his name. His writing is actually far more diverse than his reputation implies, as *Adventures of the Rat Family* attests. Verne's canon includes more than 60 novels as well as numerous plays, short stories, articles, and poems. A range of genres and literary forms is represented; science fiction actually accounts for fewer than half of his books, and most of the remainder could be loosely described as adventure, mystery, and comedy. Verne's work has been approached from a variety of ideological and methodological viewpoints, studied from political, psychological, structuralist, and mythic perspectives. Modern scholarship has increasingly recognized Verne as a compelling literary figure whose subtlety and complexity have won attention from some of the most prominent figures in contemporary theory and criticism, including Roland Barthes, Michel Foucault, Pierre Macherey, and Michel Serres.

In *Adventures of the Rat Family,* Verne utilizes the tradition of fantastic travel, as in Jonathan Swift's *Gulliver's Travels,* to take a whimsical look at various forms of life. Verne portrays a magical movement up and down the evolutionary ladder as a close-knit family of rats is transformed into various other forms of life, from mollusks to birds. The instigator of these deeds is a genie, hired by a cruel prince who desires the family's daughter, Ratine, although she loves another. Verne both recognizes and mocks the idea of evolution by having his characters change from one species to another, finally making a metamorphosis into men and women.

Although *Adventures of the Rat Family* was originally written more than a century ago, this is its first translation into English, allowing English-language readers to fully recognize what those in other countries have long understood. Verne is an author for all ages, children and adults; his ability to be read on multiple levels is one of his outstanding talents. Children follow the thrilling surfaces and the fantastic aspects of his narratives. Adults appreciate the deeper literary subtexts: characterizations, situations and motifs, satire, and the social and political commentary. This same complexity appeared in Verne's *A Fancy of Doctor Ox,* which tells how an eccentric scientist changes a moribund and moronic country village by pumping additional oxygen into the atmosphere. The townspeople suddenly become lively and agitated, and vegetables grow to unprecedented size, seeming to prove that "virtue, courage, talent, wit, imagination, all good qualities and faculties, [are] only a question of oxygen." This contrast between science and rural life is at once accessible to children but also requires more sophisticated reading to grasp fully.

The names Verne gave his characters are full of meaning. For instance, Doctor Ox's assistant is called Ygen, and together the two combine to fill the town with ox-ygen. In *Adventures of the Rat Family,* the names embody each characterization, correlating with certain phrases and words that would have been understood by French readers. The narcissistic, selfish Prince Kissador sounds like the French *qui s'adore,* meaning "who adores himself," which of course he does. The two supernatural forces stand for the power of heaven and hell. The good fairy, Firmenta, is named for the sky and heavens, the firmament. The name of the evil magician Gardafour combines two phrases: *gard,* meaning "to guard," and *four,* meaning "oven" or "furnace," with the implication of hell. Gardafour guards over hell and is really a devil.

Most amusing of all are the names given to each member of the little family of rats, along with such idols of the rats' musical culture as Rassini, Ragner, and Rassenet. The name of cousin Raté derives from the French verb *rater,* "to fail or bungle"; French students say "raté" when they have flunked an examination in school. It is a perfect name for the pitiful Raté because every time he changes from one species into another, he retains a feature of his previous form, ending with a donkey's tail when he is human. Something always fails in Raté's case, either the power of Firmenta or evolution itself, bungling each transformation. Verne was also careful to use *la famille raton* in the title of the story, a phrase that has no English equivalent. *Raton* has a diminutive quality, providing a pleasant, endearing connotation to the idea of a rat family, emphasizing the small, petlike quality that is more commonly associated with mice.

The satire evident in *Adventures of the Rat Family* is typical of Verne and runs throughout his oeuvre. For instance, Verne parodies the *Robinson Crusoe* narrative of survival on a desert island in his *School for Robinsons* (1882), in which a lad unwittingly experiences a stage-managed shipwreck, complete with uncharted island, Man Friday, and marauding beasts. In his early years in the theater, Verne acquired an often overlooked skill in comedy; many of his novels emphasize bizarre characters in unusual locales, such as *The Tribulations of a Chinese in China* (1879), *Keraban the Inflexible* (1883), *Clovis Dardentor* (1896), and *The Will of an Eccentric* (1899). Even his most famous book (and play), *Around the World in 80 Days* (1872), on one level an innocent adventure of travel, is also a parody of British insularity and imperialism, peeling away Phileas Fogg's stuffy exterior as his travel schedule goes steadily more awry.

Other facets of *Adventures of the Rat Family* also have important parallels in Verne's writing. He wrote in a typical 19th-century literary style, reflecting the influence of his two favorite authors, Edgar Allan Poe and Charles Dickens. Verne's plots are constructed on a clocklike model, with careful attention to dates, times, and seasons. Narratives are invariably loaded with information, and the descriptions in *Adventures of the Rat Family* reflect Verne's fascination with the various places visited by the rats and the different types of species they become. The metropolitan Ratopolis shows Verne's absorption with urban problems, a motif that not only appeared in his writing but had a parallel in his life; he served for many years on the town council in his adopted city of Amiens.

Adventures of the Rat Family is also an important example of Verne deviating from his own usual formula; it is his only fairy tale and one of his few pure fantasies. Most often, Verne attempted to provide rational explanations for impossible feats, giving them a basis in geography or science. An extinct volcano reveals the way for a *Journey to the Center of the Earth* (1864); a comet provides interplanetary travel in *Hector Servadac* (1877); there is an encounter with a sea serpent in *The Yarns of Jean-Marie Cabidoulin* (1901); and the alchemist discovers invisibility in *The Secret of Wilhelm Storitz* (1910). In Verne's *Sphinx of the Ice* (1897), his own sequel to Edgar Allan Poe's *Arthur Gordon Pym*, Poe's unexplained climactic white figure is transformed into a gigantic sphinx-shaped lodestone at the southern magnetic pole. (The same motif appears when the family of rats visits a marble sphinx.)

Adventures of the Rat Family had a genesis unusual for a Verne story. The idea may have had its beginning in his childhood wanderings through his hometown of Nantes. A mere hundred meters from Verne's home was a store featuring a famous painting of two cats sitting by a stream, watching—but unable to catch—a clever but old and gouty rat. His story was perhaps an homage to the painting, since the father of the family, Raton, also suffers from gout, and ultimately—and wisely—refuses to change from a rat into a man. Indeed, Verne titled the first draft of the story "The Gouty Rat." Verne empathized with Raton and saw himself as a man contented with his position in life, unlike his wife, whom he portrays as excessively concerned with status and social ambitions.

Adventures of the Rat Family was first given as part of a European lecture tour in 1887. Although initial reaction was lukewarm, the writing of the tale so delighted Verne that he enlarged it into a novella for the holiday issue in January 1891 of the fashionable Parisian journal *Le Figaro illustré,* to which he occasionally contributed. Although the speech and short story had been directed to an adult audience, the fairy-tale style read as if it were for children; *Adventures of the Rat Family* was one of Verne's few stories written in a manner so accessible to a young audience. Verne planned to include *Adventures of the Rat Family* in *Hier et demain* (Yesterday and Tomorrow), a forthcoming book of short stories and novellas written at various times throughout his career, some of them never published before. Many of Verne's short stories had previously been used to fill out shorter books, and the 1874 volume *Doctor Ox* was composed of novellas and short stories.

However, *Hier et demain* was not actually published until 1910, five years after Verne's death. It was edited by his son, Michel, who altered some of the anthology's contents from what his father had intended. *Hier et demain* was to include "Les Aventures de la Famille Raton," "Monsieur Re-Dieze et Mademoiselle Mi-bemol," "Au XXIXème siècle, Journée d'un journaliste américain en 2889," "Souvenirs d'enfance et de jeunesse," and *Le Comte de Chanteleine.* Michel deleted the latter two in favor of "La Destinée de Jean Morenas," "Le Humbug," and "L'Eternel Adam." "La Destinée de Jean Morenas" was rewritten by Michel from his father's story, "Pierre-Jean," and "Au XXIXème siècle, Journée d'un journaliste américain en 2889" was largely if not entirely by Michel, although it first appeared under the elder Verne's byline during his lifetime. "In the Year 2889" and an abridgment of "The Story of My Boyhood" had already appeared in English, respectively, in the February 1889 issue of the American intellectual journal *The Forum* and in the April 9, 1891, issue of the British magazine *The Youth's Companion.*

The extent of Michel's changes was not known until the family vaults were opened in the 1980s, when Verne's nine posthumous novels were discovered to have been rewritten by Michel and perhaps, in at least one case, originated by him. The alterations Michel made range from the addition of new characters to wholesale revisions in basic themes. Michel's politics were more radical than his father's, and his taste in science fiction more futuristic. Today, the original manuscripts of these novels and stories have been published in France by the Société Jules Verne, but none have yet appeared in English. The translation of *Adventures of the Rat Family* is taken from the version in *Le Figaro illustré,* rather than the slightly modified edition by Michel Verne in *Hier et demain.*

Michel's alterations had yet to be discovered when *Hier et demain* finally appeared in English as *Yesterday and Tomorrow* (Associated Booksellers, 1965). Though I. O. Evans capably translated portions of the book, he further rearranged and distorted its contents, and he deleted *Adventures of the Rat Family.*

In the introduction to *Yesterday and Tomorrow,* Evans justified his omission of *Adventures of the Rat Family* and another story entitled "The Humbug" by nothing more than his subjective dislike of both stories. Because *Adventures of the Rat Family* diverges from the typical preconception that Verne wrote only science fiction and adventure, Evans dismissed the story as "absurdly fantastic." Yet Evans retained "Mr. Ray Sharp and Miss Me Flat," a fantasy of a boy's nightmare that his children's choir is imprisoned in the church organ, which had a similar mode of address and intended audience as *Adventures of the Rat Family.*

This publication of *Adventures of the Rat Family* marks the first time in more than 25 years that a Verne story never before translated into English has been issued. It is appearing simultaneously with the first English translation (by Edward Baxter) of "The Humbug," included in *The Jules Verne Encyclopedia* (Scarecrow, 1993). Finally, the attenuated effort begun by I. O. Evans 30 years ago is finished, completing the translation of *Yesterday and Tomorrow* more than 80 years after its original publication. Yet why have these stories been withheld so long?

Curiously, both "The Humbug" and *Adventures of the Rat Family* reveal a problematic and contentious theme that may also have accounted for Evans's reticence: each of the stories deals with evolution. Such a theme would probably have been prohibitive for American publishers at the time *Hier et demain* first appeared in 1910, and Evans exhibited the conservative bias of that era. Though Verne was, on the surface, an obedient Catholic, he never allowed the church's teachings to dissuade him from research or the use of plots and characters foreign to Catholicism or even to general Christian belief. Verne had long been interested in, and eventually basically accepted, the idea of evolution. His 1858 play *M. de Chimpanzé* told of a chimp introduced into high society who has better manners than his bourgeois human contemporaries despite the fact that he speaks gibberish. A dreamlike episode in *Journey to the Center of the Earth* revealed the subterranean explorers discovering a giant prehistoric man shepherding a herd of mastodons. Verne also doubted the idea of "progress," scientific or otherwise: *The Eternal Adam* describes a Noah's Ark–style deluge that causes the rise and fall of human civilizations every few hundred thousand years.

Verne portrays a definite link between man and ape in his 1901 novel, *The Aerial Village,* which was translated as *The Village in the Treetops.* The survivors of a safari try to return to "civilization," moving steadily back toward a more primitive state as they lose and leave behind modern accoutrements. Their journey is a transition carrying them from their own world to the city of a "missing link" with the apes, a type of Java man. Members of the tribe, who have their own language and call themselves the Waggdis, have permanent families and an organized, well-built town located in the treetops. They exhibit what Verne seems to believe is the uniquely human trait, religion, and have their own "pope," a mad European who has reverted to a primitive state. Verne ends the novel in the same vein in which he began it, by mocking the European tendency to carve Africa into spheres of influence, indicating that the likely outcome of the visits to the

Waggdis would be their incorporation into an imperial colony.

Evans's criticism of "The Humbug" cloaked his sensitivity to the story's lampoon of American mores by claiming that it was written offhand and survived unintentionally. "The Humbug" portrays an American huckster, an unprincipled schemer and opportunist who outdoes P. T. Barnum by claiming to have unearthed the prehistoric bones of a man some 120 feet tall. Verne was fascinated with characteristics regarded as unique to the United States ("where the merchant class are the nobility"), contrasting national types through the first-person narration of a visiting Frenchman. Verne concludes by observing "that artists with no talent, singers with no voice, dancers without a leg, and jumpers without a rope would have a dismal future before them if Christopher Columbus had not discovered America." In fact, contrary to Evans's stated reason, "The Humbug" was suppressed for political reasons, and Evans perhaps feared that an English translation would offend the American audience. Just as Evans denied the anti-Catholic overtones in *The Aerial Village,* his outdated nationalistic caution had been highlighted when he deleted the sympathetic account of the Sepoy rebellion from his edition of Verne's novel of imperial India, *The Steam House* (1880). Verne's works are often controversial and remain timely many years after they were written. *The Five Hundred Millions of the Begum* (1879), which pointed out the danger of German military-industrial might, was banned by the Nazis during the occupation of France in World War II.

The fate of *Yesterday and Tomorrow* provides a typical test case of what has befallen the Frenchman even at the hands of the more enlightened publishers and editors. Ironically, while Verne became and remains America's favorite French writer, he has been poorly treated by English-language publishers. Not until he had written seven novels and become a worldwide sensation was one of Verne's books translated into English. This was in 1867, and two more years passed before another of Verne's stories came out in English and his new books started to be translated as they appeared. For the next two decades, readers of all ages and nationalities eagerly awaited every new Verne story, and he firmly established a reputation as a reliably exciting and imaginative author. By the mid-1890s, imitators were widespread. While new Verne books were published annually in France for 47 years, English-language publishers lost interest, although his earlier volumes remained as popular as ever.

Verne's later works are among the finest he ever wrote, no less imaginative and in many cases equally if not more interesting than his earlier stories. The shortsightedness of publishers during these last years of Verne's life is indicated by the fact that it took seven years for a translation of *Master of the World* (1904) to appear. One of Verne's most riveting and popular novels, it describes a combination ship-submarine-automobile-airplane. *Second Fatherland,* Verne's 1900 sequel to Johann Wyss's *Swiss Family Robinson,* did not appear until 1923. Verne's 1910 "invisible man" novel, *The Secret of Wilhelm Storitz,* was not translated until 1963 (from a drastic rewrite by Michel, not Verne's original version).

One of the factors affecting publisher attitudes during Verne's lifetime was topical: the tenor of Verne's newer works turned increasingly political and pessimistic, becoming less agreeable to English-speaking audiences. He is quite a different writer from the popular notion of the optimistic prophet of the scientific age. Verne never concentrated simply on technology but noted its effects and context, viewing science and society as inextricably related. He was far in advance of the predominating "white man's burden" themes of his contemporaries, and the motivations of Vernian characters are usually the result of political and economic forces. Verne's works were directly shaped by world conditions, highlighting such issues as nationalism, colonialism, commerce, utopianism, socialism, and individualism. He was regarded by his own grandson and biographer, Jean Jules-Verne, as an undercover revolutionary with the temperament of an anarchist. (One of the areas in which Verne was *not* progressive was in his attitude toward the position of women; in an 1893 speech to a girls' school, he urged the importance of marriage and motherhood, an attitude reflected in *Adventures of the Rat Family.*)

British and American publishers grew unwilling to present Verne's harsh views of their respective countries, and the anticipated taste of readers in the British empire market largely governed what appeared on either side of the Atlantic. Verne's approach to issues was changed to fit any bias, by altering or deleting passages potentially offensive to conservative political and religious sensibilities. For instance, the standard W. H. G. Kingston translation of *The Mysterious Island* (1875) altered the story in a propagandistic, Anglocentric manner to change Captain Nemo—revealed as an exile from India—into an admirer, instead of an enemy, of the British. The censorship grew beyond simply changing or removing controversial passages until eventually entire books were suppressed by simply not translating them into English. In 1898, *Le Superbe Orénoque* became the first of Verne's annual books not to be translated because it portrayed colonial depredations within a tale of expeditions exploring the South American river, one of them led by a young woman searching for her lost father. Similar reasons prevented the translation of three more novels, *Les Frères Kip* (1902), *Bourses de voyage* (Scholarships for Travel) (1903), and *L'Invasion de la mer* (1905), all of which had entire plots that were regarded as beyond censorship—and have still *never* appeared in English. Yet they all retained the most popular elements associated with Verne; for instance, *The Superb Orinoco, The Kip Brothers,* and *Scholarships for Travel* are exciting adventure tales of piracy, shipwreck, rescue, murder, and exploration. Some even included a tinge of science fiction. Arab customs and Western commerce clash over a plan to irrigate the Sahara Desert, but instead an earthquake intervenes in *The Invasion of the Sea.* The Kip Brothers are two sailors wrongly sentenced to a Tasmanian penal colony; after they escape, an enormous photographic blowup of a dead man's eyes reveals the identity of the real culprit. Five early Vernian works of fiction also remain untranslated, *The Count of Chanteleine* (1864), the historical romance of an oppressed minority during the French revolution, and four stories recently published in France for the first time: the gothic *A Priest in 1839* (his first novel, written in 1847 at age 19); the comedy "The Marriage of Monsieur Anselme de Telleuls" (1855); *Travelling to England and Scotland* (1862), Verne's fictionalized account of his own trip to those countries; and *Uncle Robinson* (1872), a desert island adventure.

Sadly, even those Verne books that were translated, especially the best-known titles, were rushed into publication and were poorly translated, extensively abridged, and censored. The language is mangled, transforming subtleties into platitudes, overlooking puns and double meanings. Complexity, details, and characterizations were habitually diluted, distorting motivations and bungling technical passages or omitting them altogether. For instance, one-fifth of *20,000 Leagues under the Seas* simply disappeared in Lewis Mercier's 1873 translation, yet this text has been reprinted countless times for more than 120 years. Some hacks not only deleted portions but added passages, rewriting Verne, as is the case with the translation of *Journey to the Center of the Earth* that is still most often reprinted. Many editors have further slashed and rewritten these original misrepresentations into "versions" for "young" audiences, amplifying the legend of an author more important for his general ideas than his style and content. Although most of Verne's stories received multiple translations, the most intelligent early renderings, such as those first published in the 19th century by George Munro, Routledge, Ward Locke, or Hutchinson, fell into obscurity through disuse. Hence the strange fact that the worst translations of Verne have been the most often reprinted, although better ones were equally available and are now in the public domain. That Verne's works have become classics despite these circumstances indicates their truly formidable imaginative power.

Today, the movement to restore Verne to his proper place in the pantheon of authors has featured a growing number of accurate, meticulous, and complete renderings of Verne's French into modern English. Among the works so treated are *Journey to the Center of the Earth, From the Earth to the Moon* (1865), *Around the Moon* (1869), *20,000 Leagues under the Seas, The Fur Country* (1872), *Around the World in 80 Days* (1872), "Fritt-Flacc" (1884), and *Family without a Name* (1889). These have earned a notable reputation for such translators as Willis T. Bradley, Walter James Miller, Lowell Bair, Edward Baxter, and Robert and Jacqueline Baldick. Yet effort has concentrated on these few titles (with nine different, new translations of *20,000 Leagues* alone), and much work remains to be done on the nearly 50 other Verne titles.

Before his death at age 77 in 1905, Verne had seen many of his stories come true.

The powered flight of the first heavier-than-air machine by the Wright Brothers had occurred, along with the development of motion pictures, foretold in his books *Robur the Conqueror* (1886) and *The Castle in the Carpathians* (1892), respectively. Verne may well have known that some of his own stories had already been adapted to film before his death; today movies and television, along with comic books, have become the most common way that young people become acquainted with Verne. Verne remains an influential author as successive generations discover that his stories offer not only imagination but also the first complete analysis of the problems of the modern age. The world is still confronting the issues Verne anticipated, whether the planning of cities, the use of natural resources, or the interrelated problems of technology, totalitarianism, terrorism, industrialism, and militarism. Not only did the inhabitants of the 19th and 20th centuries live the works of Jules Verne; we continue to do so as the 21st century beckons. While Verne still has much to tell us, and many stories to entertain us, only literary specialists have access to the totality of his work. Most English-language readers are given only the merest glimpse of the range and complexity of Verne's thinking, and many of his tales have been needlessly withheld. This first English translation of *Adventures of the Rat Family* demonstrates the unusual and intriguing material—valuable, historic, and in many cases controversial—that remains unavailable in English. Is it not time to finally offer *all* Verne's stories to readers, translated faithfully and completely?

EVELYN COPELAND was born in New York City and received her education in French and related studies there and in Tucson, Arizona. She is a retired teacher of French at both the university and high school levels and has also done some scientific translations. She lives in Tucson, where she does tutoring in French and in English.

IONA OPIE is a noted authority in the field of children's lore and literature. With her late husband, Peter, she has edited and written many books on children's literature and games, including *The Oxford Dictionary of Nursery Rhymes, The Oxford Book of Children's Verse, The Classic Fairy Tales,* and *The Singing Game.* Their collection of children's literature is now housed at the Bodleian Library of Oxford University.

BRIAN TAVES is senior author of *The Jules Verne Encyclopedia* (Scarecrow, 1993), which documents the influence and popularity of Verne, especially in the English-speaking world. He has been interested in Verne for more than 25 years. Taves is also preparing a book on Jules Verne and the media, a historical and theoretical account of the hundreds of adaptations of Verne for theater, movies, radio, and television from around the world. He has written extensively on film and popular culture and is the author of numerous articles as well as *Robert Florey, the French Expressionist* (Scarecrow, 1987), a biography of the noted writer-director, and *The Romance of Adventure* (University Press of Mississippi, 1993), a genre study of historical adventure movies. Taves holds a Ph.D. in cinema studies from the University of Southern California.

FELICIAN MYRBACH-RHEINFELD (1853-1940) was born in Austria. He was an officer in the Austrian army until 1881, when he moved to Paris where he began work as an illustrator. His work appeared in many popular magazines and he gained a reputation as one of the leading illustrators of his time. He worked in various European cities, winning numerous awards for his work.

THE IONA AND PETER OPIE
LIBRARY OF CHILDREN'S
LITERATURE

The Opie Library brings to a new generation an exceptional selection of children's literature, ranging from facsimiles and new editions of classic works to lost or forgotten treasures—some never before published—by eminent authors and illustrators. The series honors Iona and Peter Opie, the distinguished scholars and collectors of children's literature, continuing their lifelong mission to seek out and preserve the very best books for children.